The Powerful Nan Nee

J.A Hall

For all those who have loved, we'll live forever.

Chapter 1

You're Not Welcome Here

Rua is an area that is steeped in beauty, a beauty like you've never seen, wild in winter and peaceful in summer. Its soaring high mountains slopes cut down into deep blue lakes and vast rolling country side with large ancient oak trees and endless meadows. It's in this land you'll find a rather simple, yet usual cottage that is suited on the side of a rolling hill with a wild flower garden that is in full display as summer begins to arrive. The cottage is coated with thick green ivy which turns red in autumn and sprinkled with white flowers in spring. The ivy only allows the large oak wooden door and two small sash windows to be visible. The roof thatched with dark brown reeds was nothing out of the ordinary; in fact, the cottage would not look any different to any cottage you or I have ever seen. However, Rua is where quite magical and extraordinary series of events took place between a little girl called Ellie and her Nan called Nee.

'Oh no no no,' Nan Nee shouts as she stomps through the door chasing a red-chested hen, which had scuttled in before her. 'GET OUT, YOU! GET OUT!' she screams as the hen runs in panic around the kitchen.

Nan Nee grabs her rather bent wooden stick and bangs it angrily on the floor, while bruising her curly gray hair away from the front of her eyes to behind her ears that seem to soar above her head like misplaced skyscrapers in a flat line city.

'GET OUT, GET OUT!' Nan Nee screams again.

Ellie runs into the kitchen from the side room with her jet-black hair blowing behind her and immediately bursts into laughter.

'Nan, leave her alone.' She chuckles as she heads in the direct of the panic-stricken hen.

'I'm sick of that hen; she's nothing but a... Oh, she's next for the dinner, I'm telling you,' Nan Nee yells before being interrupted by Ellie.

'Nan, she's my hen and she's going nowhere,' she states as she calmly bends down and picks up the hen.

'Hmmm, you'll be getting no new hen for your 8th birthday, I can tell you that,' Nan Nee mutters under her breath as she puts down the stick and calmly takes a seat. Ellie puts the hen outside and shuts the door.

'Tea?' Ellie asks.

"I'd want more than tea, but, yes, that would be lovely," Nan Nee replies as she wipes her weather-beaten face.

Ellie walks to the stove and reaches for the gray stainless steel kettle. As she does, out of nowhere, "BANG" "BANG" "BANG", the loudest noise that you have ever heard explodes in the kitchen and a large flash of light blinds Nan Nee and Ellie.

4

Frightened, Nan Nee yells, 'What Now? Get down, Ellie, the place is falling down.' Nan Nee rushes from her seat and grabs Ellie pushing her to the ground in panic.

After several seconds pass, Nan Nee, dazed, picks herself from the floor and staggers to her feet. 'What the hell,' she stutters in disbelief at the sight standing before her on the kitchen table: a small human-like creature no bigger than a newborn child. The creature is dressed in a long green robe with a hood over its head and blond hair peeking out the side of the hood. The creature also carries a wooden staff which it holds tightly.

'What is it, Nan?' Ellie asks as her bight blue eyes open wide with surprise and her pale complexion gets even paler.

'It's….It's… It's…. It can't be… it's a Grolei. Can you see it too, Ellie?' Nan Nee asks out loud.

'Yes, I can,' Ellie replies.

'GO AWAY! We want nothing to do with you,' Nan Nee shouts as she straightens her back and pushes forward towards the Grolei.

'Please, I come in peace,' the Grolei replies in a deep soft voice. 'I need your help'.

'Oh no no no no,' Nan Nee replies shaking her head in disagreement.

Ellie eyes open wide and she jumps excitedly towards the Grolei, forcing it to take a few steps back unexpectedly.

'My name's Ellie. What's yours?' Ellie asks the Grolei while reaching out her hand to offer a welcoming handshake.

'Ellie!' Nan shouts and stamps her feet with temper on the hard cold stone floor and turns to Ellie. 'You don't know what these people are. They're bad news,' Nan Nee claims while pointing to the Grolei. 'I thought these creatures were myths, ancient myths. As a child, I heard stories of all the mischief and harm these creatures did to people, but I thought they were made up. Fiction, like that in the books you read, Ellie. They're bad news, I know they are.'

Then, suddenly, Nan Nee turns to the Grolei. 'What do you want from us? You're not welcome here,' she naps angrily.

The Grolei looks stunned at Nan Nee; he had expected a more friendly welcome. Perhaps his entrance should have been less dramatic, he thinks to himself; after all it has been quite a few years since a human has laid eyes on the Grolei species.

'Let him talk, Nan; at least, can we find out his name?' Ellie says taken back by Nan Nee's reaction.

'Fine. Speak, you... speak!' Nan Nee snaps again at the Grolei.

The Grolei looks at Nan Nee and Ellie and begins to speak. 'It's nice to meet you both. My name is Mugru of Cooperage wood and chief hand to Queen Elatha of Grona. As you can see, I'm indeed a Grolei and, yes, we are real, very much so.'

'Pleased to meet you. I'm Ellie, and this is my grandmother, Nan Nee' Ellie replies and walks towards Mugru to shake his hand.

Ellie's hand is so big compared to that of Mugru that he is only able to grip the top of Ellie's index finger.

'Where do you come from?' asks Ellie.

'Well, have you ever wondered what happens under your feet, Ellie?' Mugru says as he points downwards to the floor. 'Do you ever wonder what controls the underground? Well, we do! Groleis do and we come from the underground world of Grona. We have been living there for far longer than any human has roamed these parts. We control anything that comes from the ground, we decide how the plants grow, how high the trees will grow, where the rivers will run, how high the mountains will reach, when the flowers will bloom, and how good a harvest will be for those living on the overworld,' Mugru explains

Ellie looks towards Nan. 'Is this true, Nan? Have

you heard this before?' she asks.

Nan Nee nods her head in agreement. 'I've heard stories from my parents who have heard stories from their parents about the Grolei, but everyone thought they were a myth. I've never seen one, no one I know has ever seen one and I, for sure, hoped I'd never see one,' Nan says.

'They're not to be trusted. I've heard stories of them tricking humans and causing grief to whoever they met,' Nan Nee continues.

Mugru interrupts Nan Nee, 'In the past, there might have been some past issues, but we have been with peace with humans and the overworld for many years now.'

'Well, what brought you to my house?' Nan Nee asks.

'I'm here to ask for help, Nan Nee. The ruler of Grona, King Dragda, has been cast under a spell by his brother, Prince Oltar, who wants to be King. Prince Oltar wants to seize power and has vowed to end the peace with the overworld and plunge us into a terrible war. The Prince wants to bring the overworld to ruin, he believes the humans and those on the overworld are not grateful for the services the Groleis do. The Prince has already started attacking villages and killing Groleis loyal to King Dragda and has placed a spell on the King which has caused him to fall into a state where he can no longer rule. Queen Elatha has asked me to come here and ask for your help to cure King Dragda and help stop Prince Oltar from taking power in Grona and thus saving both the underworld and the overworld from destruction,' Mugru explains.

'WHAT!' Nan Nee shouts as she puts her hands in the air.

'We want nothing to do with this; this is none of our business. This is a trick. I know it is.'

'I assure you this is not a trick. Queen Elatha has asked for you personally to help.'

'This is amazing, I'm in,' Ellie says exuberantly.

'NO... no, you're not. This is a trap I know it,' Nan Nee replies.

'Queen Elatha said you might be reluctant, Nan Nee, so she has asked me to give you something.'

'I don't want it,' Nan Nee protests.

'I insist, Nan Nee. I will return later today, and if you like your gift, you might be persuaded to join us, but if not, well, then we'll see,' says Mugru.

With that, Mugru raises his wooden staff and points it to Nan Nee. A large flash of light exits from the top of the staff and hits Nan Nee knocking her to the ground. Once again, a loud bang fills the room and Mugru disappears just as quick as he had arrived.

Chapter 2

Power Takes Hold

Nan, dazed, looks around the kitchen in disbelief. She slowly tries to pick herself up from the hard wooden floor. "He knocked me," she says faintly.

Looking towards Ellie, Nan Nee slowly picks her aching body fully from the floor and in discomfort, straightens her posture. "Ellie, he knocked me to the ground in my own kitchen. My hip will never survive this." Nan Nee rubs her hip in a circular motion and groans to the sharp pain that has traveled down her hip.

'Nan,' Ellie screeches in the top of her voice and points to where Nan Nee is standing. 'You're hovering above the ground.'

Nan Nee looks down, and to her disbelief, she is hovering. "Oh, what's happening, I can't get back on the ground!" Nan Nee yells as, in a slight jumping motion, she tries to force her feet to touch the floor again.

'Oh, Ellie, what has he done to me and where the hell did he go to?'

Ellie looks on in amassment, and slowly makes her way to Nan Nee. She touches Nan Nee's shoulder and gently pushes her back on to the floor. As soon as Nan Nee's feet are back on the floor, she bounces straight back to the position she held, hovering in mid-air. Ellie, in vain, tries to get Nan Nee back onto the floor. Then, as though a bolt of lightning had struck Ellie, she jumps in the air and shouts with excitement, "I think you can fly, Nan. Mugru has given you the power to fly," Ellie says as she quickly removes her hands from Nan Nee's shoulder giving up on her efforts to get Nan Nee on firm ground.

'Try and move,' Ellie yells with excitement.

Nan Nee hesitantly tries to move by forcing her body in slight motions to the left. Suddenly, as Nan Nee shakes her body to the left, she is flung to the left with such speed she hits one of the foremost walls of the cottage with a wicked bang and slips to the floor.

'Oh!' Nan Nee moans as she slumps on the floor. 'Oh, this isn't good, Ellie.'

Ellie rushes to Nan Nee and places her arm under her shoulder and slowly lifts her up from the ground. 'Maybe try and go a bit slower this time,' Ellie says as she picks her up and Nan Nee resumes a hovering position above the ground.

'Okay, okay, let's try again,' Nan Nee says as she raises her hand to her shoulder and dusts off her knitted green cardigan. She cautiously tilts her body making a small movement to the right, and moving with ease, she glides to the right. She breaks a smile and then glides to the left.

'Yeow, we got this,' Nan Nee states as a wide grin takes over her face.

'Try to go higher, Nan. You can fly!' Ellie says.

'Oh, I don't know,' Nan Nee says nervously.

Nan Nee tries a jumping movement and shoots with great speed high into the air, so high she hits her head with a loud bang off the ceiling and hovers high above Ellie in the kitchen.

Nan Nee laughs out loud and looks down to Ellie. 'I think I've this worked out,' she says while still laughing. 'Let's take this for a ride,' Nan Nee says as she swoops down from the ceiling, bursts open the front door narrowly missing the doorframe as she swoops out into the farmyard and soars high above the countryside.

Ellie dashes out the kitchen door and looks up in amazement as Nan Nee swoops, dips and dives high in the air above the farm.

'Yahoo,' Nan Nee yells as she swoops through the air. Nan had never felt so free in all her life as the wind sweeps past her face.

She makes a sudden dart for the farmhouse and swoops down and grabs Ellie by the under arms and wraps her hands around her tiny body with a good grip.

'Ooooohhhhh!' Ellie screams.

'Look at the views, Ellie, this is amazing,' Nan Nee says as she swoops over the farmyard and lush countryside.

Below, a neighbor who is tending to their crop of potatoes in a nearby farm stands in shock as he peers to the sky to see Nan Nee and Ellie flying overhead. Nan Nee catches the neighbor's eye and swoops lower to hover over him. The neighbor, a local farmer, is dressed in an old dirty white shirt and overstained brown trousers with green wellington boots which are getting browner by the day with muck and overuse. Nan Nee dislikes the man; apparently, he is too nosey for his own good.

'How's Paddy today?' Nan Nee says and shoots off before Paddy whose mouth is open wide has a chance to answer. Ellie and Nan Nee burst into laughter as they continue to glide through the sky.

'Can you go higher?' Ellie asks.

'No, this is as high as I'm going. You probably need a license or something if you want to go higher.'

With that, Nan Nee swoops down in the direction of the farmhouse and slowly lowers herself in front of the farmhouse door and lands completely on her feet without difficultly, placing Ellie safely on the ground.

'Well, that was unexpected. Let me have that cup of tea. I'm exhausted after that flight; I might be a bit jetlagged,' Nan Nee says as she and Ellie walk through the farmhouse door bursting into more laughter.

Inside, Ellie puts the kittle on the stove and gets two cups from the cupboard.

'This is great, Nan. Work in the farm will be so easy, it's going to save hours being able to fly,' Ellie says and then breaks into uncontrollable laughter.

'Hmm.' Nan Nee exhales heavily.

Ellie makes the tea and they both sit down by the open fire and take in what has just happened. After a few moments of quiet, Ellie breaks the silence.

'Are you going to help the Grolei, Nan?'

Nan looks into her cup of tea, thinks for a while and then mutters, 'No.'

'Why, Nan? Why? They have given you amazing powers!'

Nan turns her head to look Ellie in the eye. 'No, Ellie, they can't be trusted. I've lived all my life without them and I can continue without them now,' Nan replies as she slowly moves her gaze back to the burning fire.

Suddenly, a loud knock is heard at the door, and before Ellie or Nan Nee could stand up to attempt to answer the door, an old man bursts in. Out of breath, he bends down and places both his hands on his knees momentarily while trying to catch his breath. He looks up and scans the room. It's Paddy, Nan Nee's neighbor looking very pale.

'Nan Nee, are you all right? Are you Okay?' Paddy asks in panic as he stares at both Ellie and Nan Nee.

Nan Nee stands up and straightens her shoulders. 'I'm perfectly alright, Paddy, Why?'

Paddy looks dazzled at Nan Nee. Unsure what to say, he pauses for a few moments. 'I... I ... I saw you flying through the air just a while ago. Ellie, you were flying too,' Paddy says looking towards Ellie in confusion.

'Paddy, you must be going mad. Have you taken the right medicine today?' Nan Nee replies giving a wink to Ellie as she does.

'You were flying, Nan Nee, I saw you. You even said "hello Paddy". I'm not going mad… or am I?' Paddy replies looking more confused and doubting his actions more with every second.

Nan walks towards Paddy and places her hand on his shoulder. 'Paddy, Ellie and I have been here all day, we haven't been up in no air and I don't think I was flying. Maybe you have been working too hard. Have you had any rest?' Nan Nee asks trying to hold back a grin on her face.

'I'm well. It does seem a bit mad, alright. Well, maybe I've been working too hard, the carrots won't weed themselves, you know,' Paddy replies.

'I know, I know,' Nan Nee replies mockingly.

'Maybe go home and have a rest, I think you were seeing things today, because Ellie and myself haven't left the house,' Nan Nee says as she gently leads Paddy to the front door and leads him outside.

'Go on now, I won't say anything to anyone, okay, Paddy?'

'Okay, Okay. Sorry, I must have been seeing things.'

'Maybe, Paddy,' Nan Nee replies as she watches Paddy walk down the garden path that leads to the road.

Nan Nee turns into the cottage and closes the door. Unable to control herself, she bursts into laughter. Talking quick breaths through the laughter, she utters while laughing uncontrollably, 'Oh, that was good! Oh, he'll be confused for days!'

'Why did you do that, Nan? He'll be worried he is going mad,' Ellie asks looking at Nan Nee in disbelief.

"Oh, serves him right, the nosy bugger. He only comes looking for news."

Ellie Looks at Nan Nee and busts into laughter.

Chapter 3

<u>The Arrival</u>

As the day drags on, Nan Nee becomes ever more anxious with the thought of the imminent return of Mugru. Her decision has weighed on her mind all evening. Pacing the kitchen floor, she raises her hand slowly and brushes the hair from her brow.

'Where is he? They are really dragging this out; he said he'd be back later. I need this over with. They won't like the answer, but that's it!' she says out loud reassuring herself that everything will be fine.

Ellie looks into the flames of the fire burning brightly and doesn't reply to Nan Nee to reassure her.

'It will be fine,' Nan Nee says again as she sits down at the kitchen table and places her hands over her worried face.

BANG! The kitchen fills with the loudest of bangs. The noise is so loud it causes the entire cottage to shake and a big plum of dust raises to engulf the kitchen. Nan Nee and Ellie are jolted right out of their seats, knowing that Mugru must be back. Both try to brush the plum of dust away from their faces and cough as the dust consumes them. As they are frantically trying to brush the dust away, it begins to settle and, to the shock of Nan Nee and Ellie, it's not Mugru that is standing on top of the pine kitchen table; it appears to be a female Grolei, still the same height as Mugru. The Grolei has long white flowing hair that is kept in place with a silver

21

crown which shimmers in the dull light of the cottage kitchen. The Grolei wears a long purple dress with gold embroidery which drags behind her and has a large golden pendant in the shape of a phoenix pinned to her lapel. She also holds a tall silver staff, which seems to be engraved throughout with a language both Ellie and Nan Nee has never seen before. On top of the staff is a large rounded green jewel that sparkles brightly as the light bounces off it.

'Where's Mugru? And who are you?' Nan Nee asks forcefully. 'We're expecting Mugru.'

The Grolei looks at Nan Nee and Ellie up and down and then bows her head in acknowledgement. The Grolei slowly lifts her head again and begins to speak in a low soft voice.

'I'm Queen Elatha of Grona. I've come to beg for your help, Nan Nee.'

Nan Nee looks at the Queen with a look of disdain and snaps back to Queen Elatha, 'My answer is NO, I can't help, I don't have the time, and it has nothing to do with me. Now, move along and find some other fool to do your dirty work.'

'It is not lightly I ask for your help, Nan Nee,' Queen Elatha interrupts. 'This is the first time in over 300 years that a monarch of Grona has entered this world and it is not without good reason I am here talking to you. I beg you, Nan

Nee, please listen. Grona is in very grave danger; it's a danger so grave that it chills me to the bone. The King 'King Dragda' has been placed under a wicked spell by a witch loyal to his brother, Prince Oltar and has lost his mind. Things he once knew have been forgotten, he now does not respond to anyone and is unable to give commands. His People are suffering gravely.

'The Kings brother, Oltar, is now marching with a large army on Grona, killing and attacking anyone that does not support or disagrees with him. He has burned villages and homes and is now heading to the capital.'

'What has this to do with us?' Nan Nee asks as her tone softens.

'If Oltar takes power, you'll have a lot to lose, Nan Nee. We all have. Oltar wants to start a war with the overworld to ensure you all know who is in power. He believes for too long the Groleis have been dismissed and it's time for them to run both the underworld and the overworld. He has promised to make sure nothing will grow in this overworld, the trees will no longer bud with lush green foliage, your crops will fail, the grass will turn brown, your livestock will starve, the rivers will run dry and humans will face the biggest famine that the world has even seen; many will die needlessly. If Oltar wins, we all lose, both this world and in Grona.'

Nan Nee and Ellie look at each other soberly,

both unsure how to respond.

Queen Elatha walks towards Nan Nee and reaches for her hand. Only able to grab one of Nan Nee's fingers, the queens looks at her in the eyes and pleads, 'If you fail to help us, Nan Nee, you will put everything you have now at risk of being destroyed forever. If you don't want to help me, then please do it for this world. We need you.'

Nan Nee keeps eye contact with Queen Elatha and pulls her hand back breaking the contact with the Queen. 'I don't understand, why have you come to me? There are far more people in this world that can help you. I'm just a poor farmer on the side of a hill, trying to eek a living; I'm no good to you.'

'Oh, but you are Nan Nee. You may not feel or see it, but you are the best hope we have, believe me, you are our only hope,' Queen Elatha replies.

Nan Nee, looking a bit faint, sighs and sits down, placing her elbows on the table. 'Fine, I'll help.'

Ellie walks up to Nan Nee and places her hand on her shoulder. 'We have to help them, this is the right thing to do Nan,' Ellie states.

Nan Nee nods in agreement with Ellie and looks to Queen Elatha. 'What do you want me to do?'

'I need you to come with me to Grona, Nan Nee!

I'll explain all there,' Queen Elatha replies.

'What about Ellie? She has to come with me,' Nan Nee replies abruptly.

'Grona is a dangerous place now; it's you that can only help us. I cannot guarantee Ellie's safety.'

Nan Nee angrily rises from the chair causing a screeching sound to echo though the room. 'Then NO, take away the powers Mugru gave me, I'm not going. It's me and Ellie or NOTHING!'

Ellie smiles and looks at Nan Nee.

The kitchen falls silent as Queen Elatha turns her back on Nan Nee and Ellie and walks up to the top of the table and takes a deep breath.

'Fine, Ellie can come. I must tell you, the powers Mugru gave you have no effect in Grona; they only work up here. Ellie will be given no powers; they are just for you, Nan Nee!'

'Agreed,' Nan Nee replies as she grasps Ellie by her arms and murmurs, 'If we write a book on this, they won't believe it, Ellie.'

'If we've all agreed, then follow me,' Queen Elatha states forcefully.

'HOLD UP… You want us to go now? I have a farm to tend.'

'WE'RE GOING NOW!' Queen Elatha shouts and stamps her staff vigorously on the kitchen table which results in a green bolt of light to burst from the sparkling green jewel.

The Queen in no mood for negotiations jumps from the table to the wooden stool just by the kitchen table and leaps confidently from the stool to the hard kitchen floor.

'COME, follow me,' Queen Elatha says boldly and walks out the cottage door and into the farmyard.

Nan Nee and Ellie look at each other, and Nan jokes, 'I think we better go; she's a women on a mission.'

They both follow Queen Elatha out to the farmyard and Nan Nee shuts the cottage door behind her.

Queen Elatha leads them down the path both Ellie and Nan Nee know well. The path is overgrown with lush ferns and yellow flowering gorse bushes and brambles, which leads down the left hand side of the cottage. It's where, each summer, Ellie picks blackberries and wild gooseberries. The path leads to a small pond which Ellie was always told to keep away from, and until today, she has never gone without Nan Nee by her side.

As they walk down the path, Nan Nee, unable to

resist, asks, 'Where are we going? I just thought we never bought a coat.'

Queen Elatha stops in her tracks and turns around to face Nan Nee.

'Sorry for my abrupt manner,' Queen Elatha says. 'It's just we don't have any time. You'll understand when we get to Grona. I'm bringing you to one of the entrances to the underworld. These entrances have not been used by humans for hundreds of years and must remain a secret. You must never tell anyone where the entrance is, okay?'

'Oh ya, no problem,' Nan Nee replies while nodding her head.

'Okay, it's just over here.' Queen Elatha leads Nan Nee and Ellie further down the overgrown path and comes to a sudden stop. 'Here it is,' Queen Elatha says pointing to the entrance.

Nan Nee and Ellie look at each other in shock. In all their days, they never thought this would be an entrance to the underworld. There is no grand entrance, no fan fair and no ornate decoration. What stands before them is just a large brown puddle of mud.

'I'm not going down there,' Nan Nee states. 'Oh I'm going to get destroyed. Is there no other way?'

'This is the only entrance for miles. You will not

get dirty, trust me,' Queen Elatha replies reassuringly.

'Oh, sure to hell with it, let's go,' Nan Nee replies.

'Ok, please follow me and do exactly as I do, you'll be fine,' Queen Elatha explains.

The Queen takes a step back, takes one joint leap and lands in the middle of the puddle. Boom, she disappears and vanishes into thin air. The puddle doesn't even ripple; it is like no one has even touched the puddle.

'Ok, let's do this, Ellie.' Nan Nee grabs Ellie hand. 'In 3, we jump together.'

'Okay' Ellie replies.

'Right, 1…2…3!'

Both Nan Nee and Ellie jump high into the air and land directly in the middle of the puddle and they vanish from sight.

Chapter 4

The New World

Nan Nee and Ellie are tossed and turned through a deep and seemingly endless hole of darkness. All around them is pitch black and a deafening zooming sound of speed rings through their ears. Ellie clinches on to Nan Nee's hand with all her might and screams at the top of her lungs as they fall through the unlimited darkness until suddenly there is a large flash of light, which blinds both Nan Nee and Ellie. The movement stops suddenly and they both land on their feet in darkness. Both look around in the darkness and spot a crack of light that seems to lead to daylight. Both Ellie and Nan Nee stand still and allow their eyes adjusted to the darkness.

At that moment, Queen Elatha appears in the light her outline only visible. 'Welcome to Grona, Nan Nee and Ellie. Come along. This way.'

Still holding a firm grip to each other's hand, Nan Nee and Ellie walk towards the crack in the dark room and exit to bright light. Startled by the light, both Nan Nee and Ellie squint, and to their amazement, in front of them is a vast open land, with high mountains and lakes. The trees have began to turn bright orange, there was a bright blue sky and the sounds of birds could be heard. In the near distance, a large castle stands overlooking a large town that is made up of small terrace houses. It is beautiful; it is like nothing they have ever seen before.

'This is Grona, and there is the Capital Dorinia. This is where my husband, King Dragda, and I reside.'

Ellie looks in amazement and catches a glance of her feet on the ground, which look to be a lot closer to the ground than she remembers. Ellie eyes herself up and down and then looks to Nan Nee. 'Nan, look,' she suddenly shouts. 'Look how small you are.'

Both Nan Nee and Ellie have shrunk to a quarter of their sizes. Their whole body features has changed and shrunk to the size of the Grolei. Even their clothes have shrunk to fit their new body shape.

Nan looks her body up and down, and stretches out her arms to see how far her reach has changed. She is not impressed. 'Ah, dear God, what's happened? They've shrunk us. I'm no bigger than a piglet on the farm. Oh, Ellie, you're tiny too… Oh no… What have they done to us? Oh we shouldn't have come, Ellie; I knew it!' Nan Nee squeals in panic.

'We can't go back now, Nan, we don't even know how to get back!'

Queen Elatha, unfazed by Nan Nee's outburst, continues to explain about Grona. 'Behind you is the Tree of Septirua. This is one of the three access points to your world.'

Nan and Ellie turn around slowly and, with their mouth wide opened, look at the largest tree they have ever seen. They strain their heads to look up and still can't see the top. It is a large tree of a verity, its bark is thick brown with deep crevices, and the leaves which are totally circular have turned a golden red. Where Ellie and Nan Nee stand, there is a small crack; it is the crack that Nan Nee and Ellie have just exited.

'WOW!' Ellie said as she stood in amazement.

Just as Ellie has spoken, Queen Elatha shouts the words "EETTA NA VOMMMMEL" and pointed her staff to the crack on the tree, and as she did, the tree starts to fill in as the bark slowly creeps into the empty space until it has fully sealed the crack.

'And to your left is the forest of Mlers. It's always lovely this time of year,' the Queen casually explains.

'Wait,' says Ellie. 'It's autumn here? It's just the start of summer in our land.'

'Ah, yes, Ellie, our seasons are the opposite to your world. Whens it's summer here, it's winter in your land. It's the way it has always been.'

'Oh,' Ellie replies.

'HOLD UP,' Nan Nee pipes up. 'Forget about the seasons, why the hell am I the size of a piglet?'

'You mean Grolei size, Nan Nee?'

'Well, yes, I suppose.'

'Well, Nan Nee, we couldn't have you at your normal size now, could we? You would become somewhat of an attraction. You and Ellie are the first humans to enter this world in quite some time. If you were to enter at your normal size I think you would do more harm than good.' Queen Elatha giggles.

'Why didn't you tell us before? These shocks are not good for me.'

'Now, Nan Nee, I promise this is the only shock, as once you are back in your world, you will return to your normal size, I promise.'

'Speaking of that, how the hell do we get back?'

'We will come to that, we have important work to do first.'

'Come on!' Nan Nee gasps. 'At least tell us when we can go back!'

'Nan Nee, please trust me, time is running out, do you see over there?' Queen Elatha points in the direction of the high mountains that cover the town. 'Do you see that dark plume of smoke rising in the east?'

Nan Nee and Ellie both nod in agreement.

'Well, that's how far Prince Oltar has come. That plume of smoke is the village of Brenns. He has burned it to the ground and killed and pillaged anyone loyal to the king. He is less than two days away from the capital. You see, Nan Nee, this is getting very close to being a reality, and that is why I am using you. If I had the time, I would explain everything and give you the royal tour, but I'm afraid I can't.'

'Okay, Okay,' Nan Nee replies.

'I'm sorry, it's just, this is all happening too quick.'

'I understand, but please trust me, Nan Nee, and you too, Ellie!'

'Now, please come with me, we have to get my husband. I will explain more when we get there. I think we will fly, it will be quicker, remember, Nan Nee, your powers cannot be used here, you will have to hold on to me.'

Queen Elatha stretches out both hands, and Nan Nee and Ellie grab one each. Queen Elatha kicks back and zooms up in the air. Both Nan Nee and Ellie dandle from the Queen's hands as they zoom over Grona and hover the terraced house of Dorinia. Queen Elatha slows and descends into the populated cobbled streets and lands in a large cobbled square, and to Nan Nee and Ellie's surprise, none of the other Groleis seem to notice their Queen flying with two accomplices.

They rush through the dark small cobble streets rushing past busy Grolei. They come to a sudden stop outside a small house, which has miniature windows and doors. Queen Elatha knocks hard on the oval wooden door, and several seconds pass before the door swings over and an older male Grolei stands at the door. He is different to the Groleis Nan Nee and Ellie has seen so far. He has long gray hair and a gray beard that grows down to his knees, and his long nose supports a large pair of glasses that cover half his forehead, let alone his eyes.

"Finally… come quick," the Grolei states.

Queen Elatha brushes past the old Grolei, followed by Nan and Ellie. They are lead into a room lit by candlelight and there is large wooden furniture throughout the room and a dully lit fireplace in the center of the room. The room smells of smoke and sut. In the corner of the room is a male Grolei slumped and curled up in a ball, his head is sunk into his knees as he rocks to and fro like a man possessed.

Queen Elatha walks over to the man in the corner and looks towards Nan Nee and Ellie. 'This is King Dragda, my husband; he has been like this since the spell was placed on him. He hasn't spoken in weeks and is unable to rule. He's confused and unable to make any decisions on how to handle his brother, Prince Oltar. I've been in charge for the last few weeks, we've put him to this hideout; however, as if word got out the King was unable to rule, Prince Oltar would gather more support and his brother's revolution would gather more speed. As you can see, Prince Oltar is making fast ground; he is burning villages, destroying innocent people's homes and livelihoods just in order to take over and cause a unending war with the overground.'

'Your Majesty,' the old Grolei who open the front door interrupts the quiet.

"Yes, Greattu," Queen Elatha snaps back.

'We have just got news that Prince Oltar has entered Meilish and our focus have retreated.'

'Retreated?' Queen Elatha replies

'Oh, this is bad! Thank you, Greattu.'

Queen Elatha turns to Nan Nee and Ellie. 'There's less than a day away. If they take control of the castle, we're doomed.'

Queen Elatha puts her hands to her head and sighs. After a few moments, she composes herself removing her hand from her head, takes a deep breath and looks to Nan Nee. 'I thought we would have more time, I was hoping to have more time to explain, but, Nan Nee, we need you more than ever now.'

'What do you mean?' Nan Nee replies.

'What do you want us to do? What can we possibly do down here for you?'

'Okay,' Queen Elatha says as she composes herself. 'I've a plan, but only you can take part. There is only one cure for the spell Prince Oltar has put on the King, there is a tonic, which is only made by a wise man that lives in the overground that is able to cure any spell. Only a human would be able to access the area the wise man is located. He lives in Wardel'

'Where?' Nan Nee pipes up.

'It's off the coast of Rua. It's a tiny island that is only accessible by flight. The island is surrounded by rough sea; it's never navigated by ships. No one is sure how the wise man got out there, but it's where you must go. This is why we gave you the power of flight, Nan Nee. The wise man name is Branty, and if you explain who sent you, he will help. He owes the Grolei a favor or two.'

'So! Do we have any map where we might find this place?' Nan Nee asked worryingly.

Queen Elatha walks towards the dully lit fireplace, places her hands on the mantelpiece, pulls a brown folded sheet of paper and starts to unfold it. She walks to Nan Nee while unfolding the paper. 'This in the map, Nan Nee, and here is Wardel where wise man Branty lives.'

'That's just off the coast of where we live… I've never heard or this place... are you sure?' Nan Nee asks.

'It's a special place, Nan Nee, believe me. Follow this map and you will find it.'

'Now, come quickly I will fly you back to the Tree

of Septirua and we will get you back to the overground as soon as possible.'

Queen Elatha turns to Greattu. 'Please keep an eye on him, I'll be back in no time.'

Queen Elatha rushes to the front door and gestures to Nan Nee and Ellie to follow. They scurry through the streets, back to the square they first landed. Queen Elatha reaches out her hands to Ellie and Nan Nee who grab hold of her hand tightly as the Queen takes to the air and soars above the town and back to the Tree of Septirua.

They land softly back to the Tree of Septirua, and without warning, Queen Elatha points her staff to the tree and yells, 'ERTTA NA VOMMMMEL.'

The tree starts to open again and the crack reappears in the tree.

'In you go, I'll leave the tree open for your return. Just walk inside and you will be propelled back to the overground. To return, use the same entry point. Do you understand?'

Both Ellie and Nan Nee nod in agreement.

'Okay, best of luck. We're counting on you.'

'We'll try,' Nan Nee replies as she catches Ellie's hand and walks into the Tree.

Chapter 5

A Potent Mixture

POP, a loud noise rings though the air across the green pastures on the overground as Nan Nee and Ellie appear out of thin air, back to the side of the puddle they jump into with Queen Elatha, what seems like days ago.

'Oh, I'm wrecked from all this, Ellie. Let's go back for tea,' Nan Nee says to Ellie with overdramatic pause.

'I don't think we have time for resting, Nan,' replies Ellie.

'Ah now! Sure, we'll have plenty of time. I'm an old woman, Ellie. Come on.' Nan Nee grabs Ellie by the arm and begins to pull her up the grass pathway up to the cottage.

Exhaustingly, both make it to the cottage, and Nan Nee lifts the latch from the door and swings open the front door. Nan Nee immediately heads for the couch and planks herself down making great signing noise as she does.

'Put on the Kettle, Ellie, I haven't been this wacked in years.'

Ellie, rolling her eyes, fills the gray metal kettle and places it on the warm stove. She sits down by the kitchen table looking increasingly annoyed at Nan Nee.

'We're going straight after the tea, Nan, Right?'

"Ya Ya Ya!" Nan Nee replies with dejection.

After what seemed an eternity in Ellie's eyes, the kettle boils and Ellie prepares the tea in Nan's favorite yellow flowered mug. Both sit down on the sofa and quietly sip at their tea, as the time ticks and the tea slowly turns lukewarm.

Ellie quickly gets to her feet. 'Get up now, Nan. The future of the world, as we know it, depends on you. We have to go!'

'Dear God, Ellie, I'm 74,'Nan Nee snaps back and begins to focus on the tea again.

'Get up!' Ellie shouts at the top of her lungs.

Nan Nee, shocked, looks at Elle in surprise. 'Right, right, okay, let's go! Jes. You got an itch,' she sarcastically states as she slowly pulls herself from the couch, grabs her coat from the side and walks to the front door, leaving Ellie standing in the middle of the kitchen

'Well, come on then,' Nan Nee says as she walks out the door.

Ellie grabs her coat and follows Nan Nee. Outside, the crisp winds catches their coats forcing them to close them with verger

'Okay, grab my hand,' Nan Nee states to Ellie while reaching out her hand for Ellie to grab.

Ellie grabs Nan Nee's hand with a firm grip and raps her other arm around her hip.

'Let's go,' Nan raises her body to the air and suddenly rises above the cottage below and into the dull gray sky.

'This will never get old,' Nan Nee shouts as they soar through the air.

'Ellie, get the map out of my coat.'

'What! I cant, I'll fall,' Ellie replies with a shiver of fear in her voice.

'Don't be silly I'll hold on to you.'

'Ah.' Ellie sighs as she loses grip of Nan Nee's hip and makes a reach into the deep pockets of her dark brown coat.

Ellie pulls the map from the coat and begins to struggle trying to unfold the dusty brown map.

'Where is this old man's Island, Ellie?'

'I don't know! I can't read it properly flying, you know. Why didn't we do this on the ground?'

'Ah, we're up here now. Stop complaining,' Nan Nee states and lets out a mischievous chuckle.

'Hmmm,' Ellie grunts.

Struggling to read the map, Ellie scans the map blankly, trying to figure out the marked landmarks. 'I think it's the island west off the cliffs of Tilly.'

'That's the one. I've never heard of it,' Nan Nee proclaims.

'Let's see if we can see it when we pass the cliffs.'

Ellie wraps the map up, pops it back into Nan Nee's coat, regrabs Nan Nee and both put their heads down into the strengthening wind.

They both soar, over open fields and the lush flowering meadow below, and climb higher over the mountain tops that surround the valley of Rua on to the open sea ahead.

They reach the cliffs of Tilly within minutes and both look down to admire the sheer high and enormity of the brown cliffs and the violent crashes of waves beneath.

'Can you see an island, Ellie?' Nan Nee shouts trying to be heard over the increasing wind.

'No, nothing.'

'Okay, I'm going to go further out to sea, it must be near.'

Ellie nods in agreement and hugs tighter into Nan Nee.

As they head over the choppy water below, the wind gets stronger and Nan Nee is slowed to a crawling pace. As the wind seems to become unbearable, Nan Nee seems to come to a stop with the increased wind making it harder to push forward. As they both slow in the distance, a mass of sharp rocks penetrate from the sea. As they inch closer, there are three large gray spears of gray limestone rock covered in long brown and green grass and seem to be joined by naturally formed rock bridges.

'Nan. Look. That must be it.'

'I think so, Ellie, this looks like a place a recluse would live.'

As they fly closer, the sea under them becomes choppier, and the waves appear much higher and screech loudly as they crash against the high-stoned island.

As they approach the island, Nan Nee circles the island to see any sign of life or any structures, but to her surprise there is nothing.

'Do you think this is it, Ellie? There are no houses or sign of life!'

'Let's land and see,' Ellie shouts through the strong wind.

Nan Nee scours the rocks for a flat piece of rock to land; to the north of the rocks, she spots a green patch of grass. She hovers over the green patch of grass, battling the wind lands with surprising ease.

'Right! Let's find this mad man,' Nan Nee states.

'Which way?' Ellie responds.

'Let's just walk; hopefully, there will be some signs of life.'

Both take off walking around the most northerly rock, struggling to navigate the sheer rock faces that litter the island. As they walk around, a figure appears on the opposite rock to which Nan Nee and Ellie are wondering. The figure is dark, but in the shape of a man.

Ellie spots the figure. 'Nan, look,' she shouts and points.

'That looks like our man, Ellie.'

'Hello,' Nan Nee shouts.

The figure walks into light, appearing from the shadows. The man has a slight build and is somewhat stooped over and carrying a wooden stick, he is wearing a brown flat cap and has a long untidy grey beard, and his face is smothered in deep wrinkles and looks weather beat.

The man signals to Nan Nee and Ellie to come closer. They both look at each other and walk towards the man. They have to cross a natural stone bridge, which allows them to pass to the other side. There is a sheer drop at both ends, which Nan Nee and Ellie nervously navigate. As they reach the other side, the man is standing there waiting.

He looks Nan Nee and Ellie up and down disapprovingly and, in a deep dark voice snappily, asks, 'What brought you here?'

'Well, hello to you too,' Nan Nee replies.

The old man looks at Nan Nee more disapprovingly.

'We're here looking for a man called Branty, and from the description we were given, you fit the bill,' Nan Nee says jokingly.

'Who sent you?' he angrily snaps back.

'The Queen of the Grona, Queen Elatha, and in a matter of urgency, she says you owe the Grolei a favor of two.'

'Hmm,' the old man mutters.

'I can see you flew here, is that Queen Elatha's work?' Branty asks, whose tone has softened.

'Well, apparently so, but some other small Grolei put the spell on me.'

'Right, you better come this way.'

Branty leads Nan Nee and Ellie down a set of stony stairs, which lead to large gray circular rock, taps it and it begins to roll sideways. "Come on in." Branty gestures and walks through the gap opened by the door.

Inside is cave-like, the room is made of rock, but perfectly carved and smooth like marble, there are tables and chairs all made from rock and a perfectly carved fireplace with a large fire burning which has a large pot place over it, which is billowing with steam.

'Come sit,' Branty gestures to Nan Nee and Ellie. They both obliged and sit in the stone chairs, which are particularly cold and quite hard to sit on.

'I am indeed Branty you speak of and I do indeed own the Grolei a debt. How have you become involved with the Grolei?'

'Not of our own making,' Nan Nee replies. 'They came asking for help, and we seem to be the lucky one they chose,' Nan Nee says sarcastically.

'Help for what?' Branty asks.

'Well, to cut a long story short, the land of Groleis is set to be taken over by the King's brother, who apparently is brutal and wants to start a war with the overland. He has placed a spell on the King making him weak and unfit to rule. His brother has been pillaging and killing people who are loyal to the king and is now only a day away from taking over the capital. Queen Elatha sent us here for a potion that can cure the King, a potion that only you know apparently,' Nan Nee explains.

'Oh, I see,' Branty replies. 'There in a bit of bother so.'

'A small bit,' Nan Nee replies.

'How bad is the spell?'

'Well, when we saw him, he was curled up in a ball in a rather dark room and unable to speak or function correctly. The Queen has been ruling the country in his absence.'

'Ohh, it's a Zinda spell, so they're playing with some dark magic there. Who placed the spell on the King?'

'The King's brother hired a witch; the Queen didn't explain in detail.'

'Oh, I bet you it was that Fasoc, a wicked type she is, wicked. Hmm…' Branty mutters.

'Have they not been able to cure it down in the underworld?'

'Apparently not, you are the only man, the Queen recons you are the only one that can help,' Nan Nee replies.

'Oh, Okay right, let me think, I'll have to make my strongest dose.'

'I haven't made this in long time; hopefully, I can do it correctly,' Branty says as he starts opening the stone cupboards doors and moving pots around the stony kitchen. He runs to the larder frantically removing weirdly coloured liquids in old jam jars and placing them on the table.

Nan Nee looks worryingly at Ellie. 'Do you need help?' she asks.

'No No No. I need to think.'

'Ahh Perleak, I need Perleak,' he says to himself as he runs back to the larder and places a yellow solid paste on the kitchen table. 'Right, I think I have everything. Now, let's start cooking.'

Branty grabs a large saucepan from the cupboard and bangs it on the table. 'Okay, okay,' he mutters to himself.

'Are you sure you don't need help?' Nan Nee asks again.

'No. No. No. Suh now.'

He grabs a blue colour jam jar and pours the contents into the saucepan and proceeds to open and pour different measures of the multicolored liquids until he interrupts the silence with 'aha that's it, this is it.'

'Ok, great,' Nan Nee announces. 'Can you just bottle it and we'll be gone?'

'Are you mad? No. I need to boil it, it will only work after an hour on the fire.'

Nan Nee rolls her eyes as Branty picks up the saucepan from the table, scuttles over to the fire and places the saucepan on it.

Branty slowly returns to the table and sits down alongside Ellie. 'I Hope that's it, I think it is,' Branty says questioning his recipe.

'How do you know these potions?' Nan Nee asks.

'I've learnt them, of course. They have been passed down from generation to generation. My father was good friends with the Groleis and frequently visited the underworld.'

'Have you been to the underworld?' asks Ellie.

'Yes, once, and my, what a place, it was beautiful, good memories,' Branty replies.

'And why do you owe the Groleis a favor? What have they done for you?' Ellie questions.

'Never you mind,' Branty snaps. 't's none of your business, you hear.'

Ellie and Nan Nee nod their heads aghast by Branty sudden outburst.

The room fills with silences, and the smell of the now boiling potion fills the room. The smell was potent, like the smell of rotting products, which gushed up Ellie and Nan Nee's nostrils and forced them to gag with the effects.

'Oh, that smell,' Ellie states.

'It's working. Shhh girl. The worse the smell, the stronger the potion,' Branty explains.

'Can we not open a door or window?' Nan Nee protests.

'NO. Please just be patient.'

After what seem like multipliable light years, Branty rises from the table, walks over to the fire, grabs the hot boiling saucepan from the fire and brings it back to the table. He runs to the larder and starts franticly scouring the shelves. 'Where is it, where did I put it?' he mutterers to himself

'Ah,' he shouts as he pulls a silver metal hipflask from the back of an overcrowded larder shelf. 'Now,' he states as he places the hipflask on the table, unscrews the metal top and slowly begins to pour the contents of the saucepan into the flask.
As the last of the potion enters the flack, Branty lifts the metal top from the table and screws it tightly.

'Here it is,' Branty states as he raises the flask in the air. 'Make sure the king drinks it all in one go, very important.'

Nan Nee raises her eyebrows and nods in agreement. 'Right, we can go,' she says and winks to Ellie. 'We can't delay.'

'Make sure the King takes it all, you hear?'

'Yes. Yes,' Nan Nee replies.

'And don't let anyone else get hold of this, as in the wrong hands this can be deadly.'

'Okay,' Nan Nee says as Branty hands the flask to her and she places it in the large pocket in her coat.

'Okay, let's go,' Nan Nee says and gestures to Ellie to come.

'Best of luck,' Branty mutters as he watches Ellie and Nan Nee exit out of the stony doorway and out into the wilderness of the island.

Outside, Nan nee grabs Ellie by the waist, gestures to the sky and starts to float up into the air.

Branty waves as he watches Nan Nee and Ellie disappear off into the sky above the island and across to the mainland.

Chapter 6

The Return

After a long windy journey over the sea and cliffs, Nan Nee and Ellie are once again flying over the familiar landscapes of home. It's not long after they see the old cottage nested amongst the hills. Nan Nee lands right outside the old cottage front door and makes a great sigh. 'Ah, we're home again, Ellie.'

'Ok, Nan, let's go back.'

'Already,' Nan Nee warily replies.

'NAN,' Ellie stomps, 'we have to.'

'Right. Gosh right. Let's go.'

Nan Nee grabs Ellie's hand and both make their way down the overgrown path way to the puddle Queen Elatha led them too.

At the puddle, Nan Nee and Ellie look down to the muddy waters anxiously. 'Let's hope this is the last time we'll ever have to do this, Ellie. On three, let's jump.'

'One, two, three.'

They both jump in the air and BANG they are gone from sight.

Suddenly, Nan Nee and Ellie are back in the dark tree that Queen Elatha had first brought them too, Nan Nee and Ellie creep towards the crack of light within the tree turn and head out to the land of Grona.

Once they both exit the tree, Nan Nee and Ellie are frozen in shock at the sight that they witness, the city of Dorinia in the horizon is red with flames and there is thick black smoke engulfing it.

'Oh, Nan, we're too late,' Ellie screeches.

'Oh no.' Nan Nee sighs. 'We might be too late, damn it, what will we do?'

As Ellie and Nan Nee stand and stare at each other in bemusement, they both decide they must try and find Queen Elatha who will hopefully be where they last left them in the house near the main square.

Nan Nee and Ellie head off to Dorinia by foot in search of Queen Elatha.
Once within the city walls, there is a thick blanket of smoke that engulfs their lungs causing them to cough and place their hands over their mouths. The city is a vastly different place, steeped in darkness and thick smoke with only dully lit street lights the only light that emanates. The darkness makes Nan Nee and Ellie twitch and nervous to the unknown faces that brush by them. Soldiers dressed in Blank with Gray clocks patrol the streets carrying clunky armor and solid silver swords which drag down to their knee. Peering through their dark Sallets, they look suspiciously at everyone and scan every passer by with their peering eyes.

As Nan Nee and Ellie get deeper into the city center, the number of the armed soldiers begins to dramatically increase, and both stop, due to fear, at a street corner.

Ellie looks at Nan Nee. 'What are we going to do?'
'I don't know, I'm sure that the place the Queen brought us to was around here, but where?'

'Do you think we're too late?'

'Maybe, but come on let's keep going, it must be around here.'

Nan Nee leads the way and Ellie follows reluctantly. They wander the dark and narrow streets confused and start to become completely lost and dazed in the narrow streets of Dorinia.

'Hey… You there,' a loud male voice shouts in the distance.

Nan Nee and Ellie are frozen in their step.

'Hey, who are you?'

The figure gets brighter and resembles the shape of one of the many soldiers that are patrolling the town.

'Come on, Ellie, walk fast, come on,' Nan Nee whispers loudly to Ellie.

Ellie follows Nan Nee in panic.

'STOP right there. What are you doing?' The voice gets louder and louder.

Nan Nee and Ellie now start to move in a brisk jog and rush aimlessly around the nearest corner. As they round the corner, Ellie's hand is caught in a firm grip.

'AHH, I GOT YOU!' the voice yells.

As Ellie looks back to the figure that has grabbed her, it's one of the soldiers that have been patrolling the street. Ellie leaves out a piercing scream as Nan Nee looks back in disbelief.

'Let go of her, you good for nothing piece of Ah. Let go of her,' Nan Nee shouts as she straightens her posture and stares directly at the soldier in the eye through his metal Sallet.

The soldier grabs Ellie's other hand and picks her off the ground roughly. 'You're coming with me; you look very much like a human to me. We've have been warned about you,' the soldier says.

Nan Nee's two eyes fill with panic as it dawns on her that they know who they are and have been waiting for them to return to Dorinia.

'Let her go!' Nan Nee screams and tries to grabs Ellie's legs from the soldier's firm grasp.

The soldier beckons other soldiers nearby for

57

help, and two more quickly approach.

'Go, Nan. Go,' shouts Ellie.

'No, Ellie,' Nan yells in horror.

'GOOOOO!' Ellie yells again as the soldiers approach Nan Nee.

Nan Nee, building with rage and fear, turns and runs down the narrow stone street.

Ellie's scream pierces through the thick smog as she's dragged away by the soldiers disappearing from view into the smoke-filled streets.

Chapter 7

Find the King

Nan Nee, on her own, is broken and distraught that she has lost Ellie. Pulling herself together, she realizes her only hope of getting Ellie back is finding the King and Queen. Composing herself, she starts walking slowly trough the dark lanes of Dorinia. Street by street, lane by lane, she wanders hopelessly in hope of recognizing the building she first entered along with Queen Elatha and Ellie.

After what seems a lifetime wandering the unfriendly streets of Dorinia, Nan Nee slumps to the ground and places her hands over her head in despair. 'Why did I agree to this?' Nan Nee mutters to herself, as she sits on the cold stony ground with her back to the damp stone outhouse.

Suddenly, a voice becomes audible to her. 'It's you,' the voice says as a figure dressed in black with a black hood emerges from the gray smoke and place a hand out to help Nan Nee.

Nan Nee, desperate for help, put out her hand and is pulled up to a standing pose.

'I've been looking for you, Nan Nee,' the figure says while pulling Nan Nee in the direction of the next street.

Nan Nee is uncharacteristically quiet as she is led through the streets, until they come to a halt outside a building Nan Nee now remembers.

'Oh, this is the house, oh thank you!' Nan says in

relief to the dark figure that led her here.

As the figure knocks on the door, it turns to Nan Nee. 'Do you not know who I am, Nan Nee?'

'No, but I'm glad you brought me here.'

As the door opens, the figure pulls down the hood from to reveal their face.

'Queen Elatha,' Nan Nee says quietly under her breath as she is lead into the house they had previously seen the King.

The room is still as dark and gloomily as Nan Nee has remembered.

'Nan Nee, we have been looking everywhere for you, we thought you were not going to come back. Where is Ellie? Have you left her in the overworld?'

'No.' Nan Nee sighs. 'I'm so glad to see you, she's gone; the soldiers took her. They said they have been looking for Ellie and I. How do they know we are here?'

'WHAT?' Queen Elatha screams putting her hands to her head.

'Oh no, when did they take her?'

'Not long ago. I don't know where she is.'

'We will find her, Nan Nee, they must have

figured out we would seek help from the overworld. This is Prince Oltar's work; he knows we won't go down without a fight. I promise you, Nan Nee, we will find her.'

'I hope so,' Nan Nee replies dejectedly.

'Do you have the potions?'

'Yes,' Nan Nee explains as she rumbles into her pockets and pulls out the metal hip flask filled with the potion, and hands it to Queen Elatha.

'Thank you so much. If this works we will be debited to you, Nan Nee.'

In the corner of the room, King Dragda is still curled up in the same position, rocking slowly forward and then backwards not saying a word. Queen Elatha approaches him slowly, putting her hand on his shoulder.

'King Dragda, we have got the cure,' Queen Elatha says slowly to King Dragda.

King Dragda is unresponsive. Queen Elatha unscrews the potion, grabs the King's chin and pulls it to the light.

'Open your mouth, King Dragda. Open it.'

King Dragda slowly opens his dry and crusted mouth and wraps his lips around the top of the hip flask. Queen Elatha begins to pour the potion into the King's mouth until it's completely gone.

Queen Elatha stands up and waits for the King's reaction.

After a few moments, Queen Elatha looks at Nan Nee. 'Nothing has happened. It hasn't worked. It should be instant,' Queen Elatha says in disappointment.
A deflated Queen Elatha shrugs. 'It's over, it was our only hope.'

'That damn old fool, I knew he was a doddery fool. That man knew nothing. Is there nothing we can do?' Nan Nee asks.

'He was the only one that knew the potion,' Queen Elatha responds staring at King Dragda blankly.

The room fills with a silence of despair as they all absorb the feeling of defeat.

BANG, BANG, BANG! There is an almighty knock on the door. Everyone jumps with fright at the sudden intrusion.

Queen Elatha turns her head to the door and shouts, 'Who is it?'

'Open up, it's me,' the voice explains.

'Is that the mad fool, Branty?' Nan Nee replies.

'Open it,' Queen Elatha gestures to Greattu, who has been standing by the door.

As the door is slowly opened, standing on the other side is Branty holding a different bottle of potion, with a slight grin on his face.

'Forgot the Elm Flower,' Branty states as his grin widens.

'You fool, you old fool,' Nan Nee shouts at Branty.

Nan, in shock, just stares at Branty slowly bringing herself to ask the old man, 'How did you get here?'

Branty delighted to be asked explains, 'It only came to me that I missed the Elm Flower as I watched both Nan Nee and Ellie hover above the island. Like a lightning bolt, it struck me that I missed the Elm Flower. I can't believe I forgot it. It's the most important ingredient, and without it it's as useless as giving the King tea. Once I realized, I recooked a new batch. I followed you back to the access point. I've been here before, you see. Luckily, the Tree of Septirua was still opened when I arrived. I spotted you on the street and saw you enter this house, so here I am. Apologies for the first batch, have you given the King the first potion?'

Nan Nee grabs the potion from Branty. 'Give me that, you fool. You nearly cost us the whole world as we know it, and yes we gave him the potions and you're right: a cup of tea would be better, you fool,' Nan Nee snaps back angrily.

Nan Nee looks at Queen Elatha with hope in her eyes and hands her the bottle of Potion.

'Okay, let's try this again,' Queen Elatha says while taking a deep breath. She unscrews the top of the potion bottle and slowly bends down to King Dragda.

'You need to take this cure, I promise this one will work,' Queen Elatha says to King Dragda as she lifts his head up and locks the top of the bottle over his lips and begins to pour the Potion into King Dragda's mouth. Queen Elatha empties the last drop of the potion into King Dragda's dry mouth, and slowly stands back from the King and waits.

Within seconds, King Dragda starts coughing uncontrollably. He lifts his head and scans the room. His coughing fit slowly stops and he looks down to his position on the floor. King Dragda confused slowly pulls himself up from the floor. Dazed he catchers Queen Elatha by the arms and looks her straight in the eye.

'Where am I?' King Dragda shouts. 'Where am I?'

'Your back.' Queen Elatha embraces King Dragda. 'Oh it's worked.'

King Dragda, confused and dazed, pushes back from Queen Elatha and looks around the room. 'This is not the palace! What have you done to me?'

'King Dragda, do you not remember?' Queen
Elatha asks.
'Your brother, Prince Oltar, put a dark spell on
you; you have been curled up in this state for
weeks. I didn't know what to do. Prince Oltar has
taken over the palace and our lands, he's about
to wage a ware with the overland; it's been
terrible,' Queen Elatha explains.

The King's face sinks and turns pale white. 'My
kingdom! My people!' He weeps placing his
hands on his head and falls to his knees on the
floor. He grabs Queen Elatha's silk black dress
and begins to sob into it uncontrollably.

'How has this happened?' King Dragda sobs.

Nan Nee, Branty and Greattu look to Queen
Elatha for her reaction to her sobbing husband.
Queen Elatha falls to her knees and grabs the
King close to her patting him gently on the back
for comfort.

Nan Nee looks at the pair with disgust. 'Look at
the two of you,' she states.
'Look at you, wallowing in your own self-pity.
Your kingdom, the world as we know it, is at risk
of falling apart and all you can do is cry. Get up,
you FOOLS. All that's wrong with you is, you
have never fought hard for what you want and
believe in. Well, now's your time, you still have
time to get your kingdom back. King Dragda, you
need to act like any great leader would do or is

that too much hard work for you? Because, I'll tell you something, I'm not leaving this goddamn place until I get my granddaughter back! So are you going to fight or just sit there and cry like a spoilt child?' Nan Nee yells.

The King, shocked, looks up from the floor and slowly begins to stands to his feet and walks over to Nan Nee. 'You're right, I need my kingdom back. My people need their kingdom back. This is Grona and we never quit, but first…' he turns to Queen Elatha and in a lower tone asks, "who is that woman?"

The Queen cracks a smile and says, 'She's the kingdom's hero, the powerful Nan Nee."

'Hmm.' The King shrugs unimpressed by the dressing down he just received.

'Okay, now, let's get our kingdom back,' King Dragda announces with improved vigor. 'Who can we still count on in the kingdom?'

Queen Elatha informs the King that 'there is still a faithful loyal following within the army and amongst the normal civilians that have gone into hiding. They still have faith in their King and when they hear you are back to rule again, they will rise and fight for us.'

'Numbers… I need numbers,' the King snaps.

'Enough, trust me,' Queen Elatha states.

Nan Nee Interjects, 'Hold up! What about Ellie? And how do we plan to get her?'

'Ellie would have been taken to the castle and would be in the cells, I guarantee it,' Queen Elatha explains.

'Who is Ellie?' the King asks.

'My granddaughter who has helped bring you back to life, she was captured by your brother's forces not long ago and I'm going to the castle to get her back. If your brother has hurt her he'll regret it, I tell you.'

'I see,' King Dragda says, confused by the evolving developments.

Queen Elatha walks over to Nan Nee and grabs her by the hand. 'We need to work out a plan to get the Kingdom back. Once we take back the castle we'll find Ellie in there,' Queen Elatha explains.

'Okay let's think this through,' Queen Elatha states. 'The king needs to organize an army of men to assault the castle. It's the only way we will regain power, there cannot be any other way.'

'Oh, I'm leading no army,' Nan Nee says bluntly. 'I'm getting Ellie and I'm out of here. I've done enough; I'm not waiting for the castle to be won back. Prince Oltar could be doing anything to Ellie.'

'Nan Nee, if we don't take the kingdom, you'll never see your granddaughter again,' Queen Elatha states. 'You need this kingdom back as much as we do, so please let's try and make a plan,' Queen Elatha begs.

Nan Nee with her lips tightly pouted nods her head slightly in agreement.

'Right,' says Queen Elatha. 'Let's get a plan together.'

Chapter 8

<u>The Dark Room</u>

'Bring her in,' a voice shouts from inside a large oak door.

Outside, Ellie is standing with her hands tied behind her back and two tall and heavy armed soldier at each side. They are the same soldiers that dragged her through the streets of Dorinia away from Nan Nee up too Dorinia castle. The two soldiers grab Ellie under each arm, open the solid clunky oak doors and into a large vast hall, with stained glass windows depicting landscape scenery and figures of old King and Queens of Grona. Ellie looks up to the high towering ceiling as she is dragged up to the top of the room. There seated on a large wooden throne decorated with red and white coloured roses is Prince Oltar. Dressed in dark armor, he sits with his hands crossed. His face and hands are dark with dirt, as though the Prince hasn't washed in days and his thick greasy hair isn't brushed; it appears Price Oltar is not pre occupied with appearances.

'Well, what do we have here?' Prince Oltar states. 'It seems we have been infiltrated by the human kind,' Prince Oltar says as he slowly rises from the throne and moves towards Ellie.

'Who are you?' Prince Oltar yells as he touches her face with his long index finger which is black with filth, which makes Ellie more repulsed.

Ellie, unable to hide her distaste for Prince Oltar's dirtiness, says, 'Do you ever wash? You're disgusting!'

'What did you say?' Prince Oltar yells and grabs her chin with a firm grip… 'Who are you?' he yells. 'What are your kind doing here?' he yells into Ellie's face.

Ellie's face is stiff as a result of the force of Prince Oltar's grip, but she doesn't budge an inch and calmly replies, 'I'm Ellie, and my Nan is going to flip when she finds me and finds out what you're doing to me.'

'Your Nan.' He laughs removing his grip from Ellie's jaw. 'So you haven't come alone; I knew Queen Elatha would try something like this! The fool. You're from the overground, aren't you?'

Ellie doesn't reply.

'Your kind have brought nothing but misery and hardship to the underworld, you have always taken us for granted, but NO MORE! I will unleash a period of suffering so great the overground will perish; the humans will beg us for help.
Your rivers will run dry, your crops will fail, the trees will wither, the sun will be the only thing you will see, it will scorch the land so much, it will all turn to desert and then you will learn who really rules your petty little overground.'

'I don't have time for this kid. Get her out of my sight,' Prince Oltar yells to his soldiers, and turns and heads to his thrown.

As Prince Oltar positions himself back into the throne, he calmly gestures to the soldiers. 'Put her in the cells until I decide how best I can use her,' he says with a wide smirk across his face.

Ellie is picked up by her under arms and dragged out of the great hall. While being removed from the hall Ellie, never takes her eyes off Prince Oltar and doesn't speak a word. The large door bangs loudly as they exit the hall and Ellie is led to a dark, cold and windy stairwell. 1, 2, 3, 4, 5 stairwells later, Ellie's is brought before a tall solid wooden door.

The soldier rustles with a bunch of long keys, and picking the correct key, he opens the door and pushes Ellie into the dark cold prison cell. The cell is tiny with no bed, no window, no heat and certainly no light. The door bangs shut and Ellie stands in the pitch back unable to see a thing. Then she whispers to herself, 'Nan Nee, you better find me.'

Chapter 9

The Plan

'How many men are still loyal?' King Dragda asks directing his posture to Queen Elatha as Nan Nee and Branty sit quietly waiting for a detailed plan to emerge from the King and Queen.

'General Remon and General Sibein have gone into hiding, I've spoken to them and said the majority of the army are still loyal and will fight for the kingdom,' Queen Elatha replies.

'Damn, I need number... how many?'

'I don't know.' Queen Elatha replies. 'Both generals assured me there will be enough; they will gather everyone willing to fight when we have a plan and give the signal.'

'Okay, we will have to trust them. Gather the remaining troops and storm the castle as soon as possible; the element of surprise will be our greatest weapon. Do the generals have the correct armor and weapons?'

'He has assured me he has everything; they stockpiled large supply of the army weapons in a store house west of Dorinia. They began stockpiling days before army entered the city,' Queen Elatha explains.

'If this is true, we need to give the signal. We will storm the castle tonight. Send a signal to the two generals at once. We attack at midnight. Exactly when he won't expect it.' King Dragda bangs the table with vigor at the thought of bringing down his brother.

'So what about Ellie?' Nan Nee interrupts.

"Yes, Nan Nee," King Dragda states.

Queen Elatha turns to Nan Nee. 'Branty, you and I will enter the castle this evening and find Ellie before Prince Oltar has any time to do anything to her!'

'And how will we do that?' Nan Nee asks.

'I know a secret passage that will bring us into the castle, and from there we can only hope we find Ellie.'

'Amm you want me to come and help find Ellie? I really don't think I should be the one, to be honest; I think I should be heading back home,' Branty says interrupting Nan Nee and the Queen.

'WHAT?' Nan Nee shouts as she stands up from her chair.

'Well, you're coming, whether you like it or not. You fool, you nearly cost us everything by giving us the wrong potion, you'll be coming with us; it's the least you can do.'

Branty looks up at Nan Nee, and immediately sinks his head back down and quietly mutters, 'Okay, I suppose I could join for a bit.'

'Hmm, you better,' Nan Nee replies.

'Great! I'm glad we were able to reach a consensus.' Queen Elatha gestures to Greattu who has been sitting patiently by the door waiting for the latest knock. 'Go give the single, we attack at midnight," Queen Elatha tells Greattu

Greattu nods in agreement, grabs his long dark coat from the chair and leaves.

'Ok, you ready Nan Nee?' Queen Elatha asks. 'It's time we should head, and hopefully find Ellie before the attack on the castle.'

Queen Elatha turns to King Dragda. 'Be careful, tonight, we'll rule again,' Queen Elatha says as she leans over and grabs the King's hand.

'Ok, we need to go,' Queen Elatha states as she pulls her hand away from the King. 'Grab one of the hooded coats from the fire side, we need to keep a low profile walking the streets tonight.'

Nan Nee, Branty and the Queen all bid farewell to King Dragda and exit via the front door into the dark fog filled streets of Duran

Queen Elatha leads them down a narrow street past the main square and down to the lake shore where the castle stands mystically above. Queen Elatha suddenly brings them to a stop, turns back and whispers, 'We're here.'

'What?' says Nan Nee. 'There's no passage

here, we're at the side of a lake. Have you gone crazy?'

'Trust me, Nan Nee, the secret passage is right here. The castle has quite a few secret passages only the King and I know. I was only told of it the day I married the King.'

Nan smiles. 'Why on the day of your wedding? Were you planning an escape?' Nan can't help herself and laughs out loud

'No,' Queen Elatha speedy replays.

'As Queen, I was given all the secrets, passages and all sensitive information. I know as mush as the King, except I don't have the power.'

'Would you not like the power? The King hasn't been ruling for some time?' Branty asks

'The King is a good man, believe me. Ever since the spell, he just hasn't been anywhere near the man I married. I promise when he returns to the throne, he will show everyone what a leader he is.'

'Ya,' Nan Nee snaps. 'Let's get into this castle, we don't have time.' She begins to walk further towards the castle.

Queen Elatha grabs Nan Nee by the hand and brings her to a halt. 'We're here!' she states again.

'Where is the secret passage?' Branty asks inquisitively.

'It's right in front of you,' Queen Elatha says confidently.

Nan Nee and Branty look at each other confusingly.

At that moment, Queen Elatha reaches into her cloak and removes a bright silver twig. She grabs the twig by both hands and snaps it in two. The noise of the snap is severely high-pitched, causing Nan Nee and Branty to cover their ears. Suddenly, the earth beneath their feet begins to shake violently all around them, and then, as if out of nowhere, a creature Nan Nee or Branty has never seen pops up from the ground looking playfully back at them. The creature is as small as mouse but stands on two legs and has a head that is twisted like the top of a drill.

Queen Elatha then whispers 'Callificia yo hoged.' The creature suddenly leaps in the air, and dives head first back into the ground and disappears.

A few moments pass before the ground begins to violently shake again. Slowly, a large wooden door rises from the earth appearing right before them.

Queen Elatha walks towards the door, turns the gold brass door handle and gestures to Nan Nee and Branty. 'Come on, let's go,' Queen Elatha says as she walks through the door.

Nan and Branty are speechless. They look at each other in confusion and enter the door after Queen Elatha.

'What was that?' asks Nan Nee.

'That was a Pero, they guard our secret doors,' the Queen states.

'Oh,' Nan Nee replies as the door slams behind them.

Chapter 10

The King's Plan

King Dragda, covered by a dark hooded cloak, nears the outskirts of Dorinia and stops in front of 'Farle Due Ru' an ancient hall which has stood in Dorinia for centuries, King Dragda nears the large green door and bangs it loudly three times. A moment passes and the door is flung open. King Dragda steps in, and to his surprise, the ancient hall is packed with soldiers dressed in full military uniform and armed.

'Ah King Dragda, I knew you'd come,' says a stout man that puts out his hand to welcome King Dragda.

'General Remon, I am very glad to see you,' King Dragda states as he grasps General Remon's hand with vigor.

'These are the loyal men who are willing to fight for you. There are over a thousand men here and we have another seven or so hundred waiting for the signal.'

King Dragda, shocked by the large numbers of loyal soldiers, looks at the general in delight. 'That many? Oh, General, I'm humbled, thank you.'

'Don't thank me, these men want to fight for what is right. Your brother has done some terrible things to people in the villages he has captured on the way to the capital, and we don't want to see what he will do now that he has full power,' General Remon explains

'Thank you, General. If I have it my way, his reign will not last long.'

'Your Majesty, I have some urgent news though. We believe our actions have been watched closely by spies. When I got your signal earlier, I got the men to prepare for battle, and in our efforts to stay low and out of sight, I worry we have been spotted by Prince Oltar's spies and troops. We need to march now, if we want to hit Prince Oltar when he least expects it,' General Remon explains while staring King Dragda in the eye.

'I see, I've made a promise not to attack the castle until midnight. Queen Elatha is on a special mission to rescue a prisoner before we attack. I cannot risk the Queen's life like that,' King Dragda explains.

'Your Majesty, with all due respect, we need to march now. Prince Oltar will have got wind of our preparations by now, and will probably be mobilizing his troops as we speak. The more time we wait, the less chance we have of succeeding.'

'I know, I know General Remon, but Queen Elatha?'

'We have to march now, Your Majesty,' General Remon says with increased vigor.

King Dragda remains silent for a few moments and takes a deep breath. 'We march now; give the signal to the other men. The men here in the great hall will march behind me, get the cannons, we leave now,' King Dragda says as he turns to the soldiers gathered in the great hall. He puts his hand in the air and the hall descends to silence.

'Brave men of Grona, we are in very grave times, evil has spread across our land and threatens everything we stand for as a people. Tonight, we fight for peace, for dignity and for justice. We will take back Doran from the evil that has darkened our land. Tonight, you become the heroes of our time, so come follow me and march to overthrow the tyrant that has cast this long shadow. Grona forever, Grona for greatness,' the King passionately shouts to the crowed

The soldiers, bursting with pride, shout back, 'Grona forever, Grona for greatness,'

Kings Dragda nods to General Remon and shouts, 'LET'S GO!'

Chapter 11

The Escape

Queen Elatha, Nana Nee and Branty are nearing the end of the secret passage; the only light to guide them is the glow from Queen Elatha's staff.

'Ok, this is the spot,' Queen Elatha states. 'Now, please don't be alarmed at what is about to happen and where we arrive at, okay?'

'What?' asks Nan Nee, but suddenly before she had time to think, their bodies are propelled from the ground and they shoot right up into the roof of the passageway where everything goes dark. Seconds pass until there is terrible noise of what sounds like pots being flung and women's screams of fear.

All three have landed in a large room full of dust, and as they begin to brush off the dust, it seems they have landed in a large kitchen with very worried-looking maids and chefs all looking at them with disbelief and shock.

Queen Elatha quickly moves to reassure them they are in no danger. 'Please, please don't say a word, I'm back to take back the castle and the kingdom.' The kitchen staff look bemused, but nod in agreement.

'They looked shocked,' Nan Nee says.

'Well, we did just shoot up out of the stove, the passage entrance and exit is via the hobs on the stove. We must of caused quite the site,' Queen Elatha says as she grins with delight. 'Come this way, this is where Ellie will be kept.'

Queen Elatha leads them into a wide open corridor and down steep steps as they move like shadows in the night in their dark cloaks. As they descend the staircase, the light fades and the surroundings become darker and darker.

Queen Elatha brings them to a sudden stop. 'The cells are just here, there may be soldiers guarding the cells if they are holding someone important. Come quietly,' Queen Elatha says as she jesters them to move slowly

As they reach the end of the staircase, in front of them are several wooden doors down a long dark corridor, the place is in near full darkness except for the dull flicker of candlelight.

'Okay, good, there are no guards,' Queen Elatha states as she looks back at Nan Nee and Branty.

'Good,' says Nan Nee. 'Actually, how are we going to open these cell doors?'

'Ah ha I was waiting for you to ask.' Queen Elatha reaches into her black cloak and pulls out a bright long silver key. 'The master Key,' Queen Elatha states as she showed Nan Nee and Branty.

'When the spell was put on the King, it was the first item I took from the castle. I knew it would come in handy if the King or I were caught by Prince Oltar's forces.'

'Right, let's start,' Queen Elatha walks to the first cell door and tries the key in the lock. After nervously fidgeting with the lock for a few moments, the door opens and Queen Elatha peers in. Nan Nee pushes the Queen out of the way and shouts "Ellie" into the dark empty cell.

'She's not here.' Nan Nee sobs.

'Come on, next ones,' Nan Nee orders.

Queen Elatha hurries to the next cell door and opens it in the same fashion; however, Ellie or any evidence of her is nowhere to be seen.

One door at a time, they diligently search each of the cells until they are at the last cell door.

'She'll be in here, I feel it,' Branty states.

Queen Elatha puts the key in the lock and the door swings open.

Nan Nee rushes in and falls to her knees. 'She's not here.' She sobs with grief.
'Where is she? She can't be gone,' she says as she puts her hands to her face.

Queen Elatha and Branty look at each other, stunned in silence.

Queen Elatha bends down and places her hand on Nan Nee's shoulder. 'Nan Nee, come on, we must keep searching.'

'Where... Where, god damnit? You said she would be here.'

'I bet she was, but we may have been too late,' Queen Elatha says as she is interrupted mid sentences by the most ferocious bang. The whole castle shakes beneath them and in the distance military horns are heard blowing.

'Oh no, we're too late, King Dragda has launched the attack.'

Nan Nee gets to her feet quickly as if the bang has knocked her back to reality. 'We have to find her,' she says as she straightens herself and looks directly at Queen Elatha.

'Nan Nee, it's too dangerous. King Dragda is bombing the castle; the place could fall down around us.'

'We're finding Ellie,' Nan Nee shouts. 'I'll do it myself, if you won't help me.'

'Nan Nee, we are in grave danger. The cannons could kill us,' Queen Elatha states trying to calm Nan Nee down.

'I don't care, she's all I got and I'm not leaving this building without her. You promised you'd find her,' Nan Nee snaps back angrily now staring at Queen Elatha with contempt.

'I did,' Queen Elatha says quietly lowering her

head almost shamefully.

'Well then,' Nan Nee says.

'Prince Oltar will probably have Ellie in the great hall. He must have seen the troops marching to the castle and knew Ellie must be connected to the King in some way. He's going to use her as a pawn,' Queen Elatha explains as she paces the cell trying to come to terms with the situation.

'To the great hall then, let's go,' Nan Nee says franticly.

'Hold on, Nan Nee, this will be very dangerous. If we're captured, only God knows what he will do to us,' Queen Elatha says as she tries to process a plan in her head.

'I don't care, he could be doing anything to Ellie now, we need to go.'

'Are you sure we should do this?' Branty pips up quietly.

'Yes,' Nan Nee snaps back, 'and you're helping,' Nan Nee says as she gives Branty a look that could kill.

'OK, let's go to the great hall and see what the situation is up there. I don't know how we are going to get in, but let's see. This is utter madness, you know,' Queen Elatha states.

'Madness, just the way I like it,' Nan Nee states

as a cheeky grin engulfs her cheeks.

'Right, follow me, stay close and keep the hood of your cloak up,' Queen Elatha states as the rush down the long corridor up the staircase they had descend moments before.

Within moments, there are back up the corridor they had taken the stairs from. The Queen looks back to Nan Nee and Branty. 'The great hall is up here, at the end of this corridor. It's on the left. We need to sneak quietly to see if it's guarded, ok? Let's go quietly,' Queen Elatha states as Nan Nee and Branty nod in agreement.

The three slowly move up to the end of the corridor. Each step is trodded gently with no one making any noise. At the end of the corridor, Queen Elatha puts out her hand up for Nan Nee and Branty to stop.

Queen Elatha slowly peers around the corner of the corridor. Before her she see two well-armed soldiers guarding the great hall door. As she peers over, one of the soldiers catches the Queen peering over the corner. She quickly pulls her head back.

'Who goes there?' the soldier shouts.

'Damn, oh damn, he saw me,' Queen Elatha whispers to Nan Nee and Branty.'

They are all frozen in fear

'Oh what will we do?'

'Show yourself,' the soldier shouts.

'Okay, screw this, follow me and say nothing. I'm going to do something I never thought I'd ever do. Queen Elatha turns to walk around the corner and gestures to Nan Nee and Branty to follow.

They both follow nervously.

As Queen Elatha rounds the corner, she removes the hood of her cloak and looks directly to the two soldiers.

The two soldiers move closer to Queen Elatha, Nan Nee and Branty

'Well, what have we here,' one of the soldiers says as he smirks at the sight in front of him.

'I am Queen Elatha, the Queen of Grona and the rightful owner of this castle.'

The two soldiers look at each other, grin and start to laugh

'Prince Oltar is going to love this. Come on, Queenie, you're coming with us,' one of the soldier says as they point their spears at them and move closer to reprimand Queen Elatha, Nan Nee and Branty.

'I will not go with you; leave now or face the

consequences,' Queen Elatha says as she removes her staff from inside her cloak.

'Leave where, Queenie? You're Queen no more. You're going to pay Prince Oltar a little visit. He's going to love this surprise,' One of the soldiers states.

'No,' Queen Elatha shouts.

At that moment, the Queen raises her staff in the air, faces it towards the two soldiers and shouts, "Fellim e Nabracha."

The soldiers are immediately frozen mid step. They can neither blink, move nor talk.

'What have you done?' Branty asks in shock.

'It's a freezing spell. I have the power to do such dark magic, although I swore I would never use it,' Queen Elatha says with regret.

'When I raise my staff and utter those words, anyone I point at is immediately frozen. It's a terrible curse. There isn't even a cure for the spell. I took an oath to never use such dark magic.'

'It's okay, Queen Elatha, you've saved us. You've done good really,' Nan Nee says attempting to reassure the Queen.

'That doesn't matter; it's still dark magic.'

'Come on. You can worry about that later, we need to get to Ellie before it's too late,' Nan Nee says as the castle is shook by another cannon and is consumed by a terrible bang.

Queen Elatha walks past the two guards and stops in front of the great hall door.

'I'm going to peer inside,' the Queen says as she looks at Nan Nee and Branty.

'Be a little bit more subtle this time maybe?' Nan Nee replies jokingly.

Queen Elatha gives a slight grin and pushes the knob of the door just slightly. As she does the castle is hit by another cannon and dust and debris fall, and as it does the Queen get the door slightly ajar.

Queen Elatha removes her hand from the door knob and bends down to peer through the gap in the door. She scans the room. Prince Oltar is sitting at a table with 5 or 6 what look like General of the Army. Prince Oltar is shouting loudly, 'Get more men, we need more.' The King's throne at the top of the great hall is empty, but to the left of the throne is Ellie, on her knees, looking tired and weary. Around the hall, several soldiers are stationed with spears in their hands looking intently at what's going on at the table.

Queen Elatha pulls back immediately, takes a step back from the great hall door and look at Nan Nee. 'It's Ellie, she's there,' she says with a sigh of relief.

Nan Nee's eyes light up. 'Oh, thank heaven. Does she look okay?'

'Yes, but she is heavily guarded and Prince Oltar and his generals are planning what their next move will be.'

'Come this way we need a plan,' Queen Elatha leads them to a small room off the corridor. They enter and shut the door behind them.

'How do we get her out unharmed?' Queen Elatha asks.

'The King has launched his attack; it may take several hours for him to retake the castle.'

'That's too late; he'll do something with Ellie. He knows we'll be looking for her and if he sees the two soldiers frozen in time, he will know, soon enough, who was behind that,' Nan Nee states.

'Use your power Queen Elatha,' Branty says.

'No… no… no… not again. If I use them in the room, Ellie will be frozen too. I can't pick and choose who gets frozen; it is whoever is in the direction of my staff. The magic is indiscriminate, as you've seen already.'

'Oh,' Branty says, 'there may be a cure though, right?'

'As far as I know there isn't, this dark magic is not practiced here.'

'Do it,' Nan Nee says, as she looks at the Queen. 'Do your magic, it's the only way we'll find a cure for it. We've come this far; we'll find a solution. Do it.'

'I can't, Nan Nee. She'll be stuck like that forever.'

'She won't, do it! Come on.'

'No, Nan Nee,' Queen Elatha pleads. 'Don't make me do that to Ellie.'

'Do it, it will end Prince Oltar as well, the war will be over and we'll have saved your kingdom as well as the overground,' Nan Nee says in a defiant tone.

'Nan Nee,' Queen Elatha says putting her two hands on Nan Nee's shoulders. They embrace and they both begin to weep.

Branty looks on as his eyes well up at the enormity of the decision.

Nan Nee gently pushes Queen Elatha off her and somberly says, 'Let's go, we need to do this.'

The all gather themselves, they exit the room and make their way to the great hall door, the sound of cannons banging echo across the castle again.

They all stand at the great hall door. Queen Elatha looks at Nan Nee and says, 'Are you sure?'

Nan Nee nods in agreement.

Queen Elatha pushes the great hall door open with great force, capturing the attention of all in the hall. She begins to walk in followed by Nan Nee and Branty.

There is a gasp in the great hall as the soldiers, generals and Prince Oltar see that Queen Elatha has returned to the castle unarmed.

Ellie eyes fill with delight and screams "Nan" at the top of her lungs. Nan Nee notices and smiles back.

'Well, look who we have here,' Prince Oltar states as he stands up from the table in shock at the sight that is before him.

'Surrender now, Oltar and it all finishes here,' Queen Elatha states as she stares directly at Prince Oltar.

'Or what, Elatha? Are you and your army of oldies going to kill us all?'

'Surrender now or else, Oltar?' Queen Elatha demands.

'You're a bit too early. Your husband is still trying

to get into the castle and you're in here, why is that Elatha?' Prince Oltar says as he turns and faces Ellie.

'Maybe it has to do with this little treasure,' Prince Oltar climbs the steps to the throne where Ellie is kneeling and places his hand on her head.

'Leave her alone,' Nan Nee shouts.

'Will you surrender or not, Oltar?' the Queen shouts angrily at Prince Oltar.

'NEVER to you, you're not fit to be a Queen or your husband a King. You've destroyed our kingdom by letting the overworld not pay for the work we do for it. This kingdom will be mine forever.'

The Queen reaches inside her cloak, removes her staff, raises it in the air and points it at Prince Oltar.

Prince Oltar eyes widen with surprise and the generals and soldiers look bemused.

'Fellim e Nabracha,' Queen Elatha shouts as she points her staff around the room to the generals, soldiers and Prince Oltar. The room is brought to complete stillness and the silences that descends is deafening.

Prince Oltar is frozen solid along with the general and soldiers.

Nan Nee rushes past Queen Elatha and heads straight up to Ellie who's completely frozen. 'Ellie,' she sobs as Nan Nee puts her hands around her and sobs into the frozen statue Ellie has become.

'My poor Ellie, I'm so sorry.' Nan Nee weeps.

Branty approaches Nan Nee and puts his hand on her shoulder. 'I'm sorry, Nan Nee. I'm so sorry.' They both just stand in silences.

Queen Elatha walks to the great hall window and pulls out a golden-shaped ball which appears to be engraved with ancient writing from her cloak. Queen Elatha pulls open one of the stained-glass panels and throws the golden ball outside. Once the ball hits the outside air, it burst into bright red and green colours.

'King Dragda will stop the attack on the castle now. The war is over,' Queen Elatha says as she walks over to Nan Nee. 'You've paid the ultimate price for all of our freedom; we are forever undented to you, Nan Nee.'

Nan Nee lets go of Ellie and steps back from her frozen body.

'Wait,' Nan Nee says, 'do you still have some of the potion we gave the King earlier?' Nan Nee asks Branty.

'Yes, I've a small mixture. I kept some back in

case there wasn't enough for the King, but, Nan Nee, that is a potion for curing a madness cure; it won't work.'

'Give it to me!' Nan Nee demands.

Branty reaches inside the collar of his shirt and pulls out a small bottle which is attached to a nylon string that he has around his neck. Branty pulls the string over his head and hands the miniature bottle to Nan Nee.

Nan Nee unscrews the bottle and walks over to Ellie's frozen body. Nan Nee tries to open her mouth a little, but it's frozen like rock. In desperation, she pours a little on Ellie's lips and continues to slowly pour the potion on Ellie's lip until it's all gone.
However, Ellie does not move.

Branty reaches for Nan Nee and says, 'It won't work, Nan Nee. Sorry.'

Nan Nee sighs and admits defeat. 'I thought it would work.'

Nan Nee turns to walk away, her head bowed down as tears roll down from her face. At that very moment, Ellie's eyes blink.

'AHHHHHHH,' Branty shouts as he pints at Ellie.

Nan Nee looks backs and sees Ellie blink once more.

'Ellie, oh Ellie,' she screams and rushes to her. 'Can you hear us? Oh, Ellie.'

'Yes, Nan, I can,' Ellie replies.

'Oh, Ellie,' Nan Nee says and wraps her hands around Ellie's warming body.

'I can't feel my arms or legs though, Nan.'

'Oh, wait, I can feel my left arm is back,' Ellie states as she waves her hand.

'You're coming back,' Nan Nee yells with excitement.

'Ellie, you're back. Oh, this is the best! Branty, that potion is amazing,' Queen Elatha announces as she hugs Ellie.

'Branty, thank you so much,' Nan Nee says as she stops hugging Ellie and wraps her arms around him.

'How can I repay you? You've saved Ellie.'

Branty, unsure how to react to the display with affection, pats Nan Nee on the back. 'It's okay. I didn't know the potion works as an anti-freeze, yet another use has been found for it,' Branty replies with renewed joy.

'I don't care; you've saved her,' Nan Nee says as she removes her embrace and turns to Ellie.

Ellie is now full defrosted and able to move all her limbs. She walks over to Branty and gives him a warm embrace. Ellie gestures to Nan Nee and Queen Elatha to join. They all embrace.

Nan Nee pulls back from the embrace and looks at the Queen. 'What are you going to do with Prince Oltar and the frozen soldiers?'

'Good Question, Nan Nee, I think a little more time frozen like this will not do anyone any harm.'

Nan Nee grins back at the Queen. 'I suppose not.'

They both chuckle.

Chapter 12

Home Sweet Home

One Month Later.

Nan Nee and Ellie are back in the familiar surroundings of the cottage in Rua. It's now mid-summer, and the long peaceful summer has to take over the land.

Sitting in the kitchen, both Nan Nee and Ellie are sipping tea by the quenched and empty fireplace. There is a rattling noise at the door and a white envelope is pushed through the letter box landing softly on the kitchen floor.

'Ellie, get that, will you? It's odd getting post now,' Nan Nee says and Ellie rises from the chair, walks to the door and picks up the letter.

'It's addressed to you, Nan Nee.'

'This is odd, post on a Saturday. Here, hand it to me,' Nan Nee says.

Ellie walks to Nan Nee and hands her the letter. Nan Nee Quickly opens the letter, taking no regard for neatness. Inside, the letter reads:

Dear Nan Nee and Ellie,

By the order of His Royal Majesty, King Dragda of Grona and Her Royal Majesty, Queen Elatha of Grona, I am delighted to inform you both that you have been awarded the honor of "The Most Ancient and Most Noble Order of Grona," for your great and heroic service to the people of Grona.

His Majesty requests your pleasure to attend a gala dinner in your honor on the 10th August at 8pm sharp.

Yours truly,
King Dragda of Grona

'Well, Ellie, we're being knighted.' Nan Nee smiles proudly and burst into laughter. 'Who would have thought of us getting knighted?'

'This is great news, Nan Nee. We get to go back to Grona.'

'Oh no, not down the damn puddle again.'

'It will be great, Nan Nee. Imagine a whole event, just for us,' Ellie says.

'It's the least they could do!' Nan Nee says jokingly. 'They nearly killed us.'

They both burst into laughter.

'I wish that puddle would dry up,' Nan Nee says through the laughter.

'Nan, whatever happened to Prince Oltar?'

'The Queen said they banished him to a dark cold corner of Grona, and he is never to return again.'

'Lucky the old man's potion worked on them too,' says Nan Nee.

'Hmm true,' Ellie replies.

'Right, Ellie, I feel we should take a trip into town. We need a new outfit now, oh, and we can get some nice buns at Kate's Bakery to celebrate.'

'Oh, yes, please!' replies Ellie.

'Right, Ellie, get your coat. We're flying today; I'm not waiting for that community bus.'

Ellie grabs her coat from the coat stand and they both walk out the cottage door.
Ellie grabs Nan Nee's waist, Nan Nee raises her hand to the sky and they both lift off into the air and over the lush green countryside below.

The End.

107

Printed in Poland
by Amazon Fulfillment
Poland Sp. z o.o., Wrocław